Shoo Rayner

Shoo began his career as an illustrator in a garden shed near Machynlleth. He drew for Michael Morpurgo and Rose Impey, but people kept encouraging him to write. Many years and more than 175 books later, Shoo has built a worldwide following for his award-winning how-to-draw videos on YouTube. http://www.shoorayner.com/

Shoo lives in the Forest of Dean with his wife and three cats.

Shoo's first book about Harri and Tân, *Dragon Gold*, was highly commended by the Tir na n'Og award 2015.

Dragon White

For Dragon Lovers Everywhere

First published in 2015
by Firefly Press
25 Gabalfa Road, Llandaff North, Cardiff, CF14 2JJ
www.fireflypress.co.uk

A CIP catalogue record of this book is available from the British Library.

Print ISBN: 9781910080306
Epub ISBN: 9781910080313

This book has been published with the support of the Welsh Books Council.

Typeset by: Elaine Sharples
Cover design by liz@madappledesigns.co.uk
Printed and bound by: Bell and Bain, Glasgow

Dragon White

Shoo Rayner

Firefly

Chapter One

Harri

'Hey, Ryan! Look at this one!' Harri waved an enormous purple-brown, wriggling, squirming, slimy worm in front of his friend's face.

'Eugh!' Ryan recoiled in horror. 'I don't know how you can touch them!'

'They're Tân's favourite,' Harri laughed, lifting the lid of a plastic tub and adding the worm to the writhing collection he'd already dug out of the compost heap at the bottom of the garden.

'If Tân is going to behave himself today, we're going to need some treats to keep him happy.'

A butterfly flitted lazily through the air and landed on the garden path. It spread its wings out to catch the warm, spring sunshine.

Whoosh! A bright red dragon swooped down from the gable end of the shed. Its fierce eyes

1

focussed on the butterfly like laser beams. Its flashing claws unsheathed just as the insect escaped into the air.

The dragon hit the ground hard. It rolled over two or three times and came to a stop, upside down, tangled in a prickly shrub.

Pulling itself free, the little dragon shook his head and shrugged its wings as if nothing had happened. A wave of motion rippled down its long, snake-like body. Then it flapped its wings and flew back to its perch on the roof of the shed to keep watch on its back garden territory.

'He's amazing!' sighed Ryan. 'He's so funny, he's like a little puppy! You're so lucky, Harri. I wish I had a dragon of my own.'

'Be careful what you wish for!' said a voice behind them. An old lady stood at the back door. 'Dragons are quite a handful, aren't they, Harri?' Her eyes twinkled.

Imelda Spelltravers had been living at Harri's

since Tân hatched from the egg she'd given him. Harri felt like she'd been living with them for years. He was starting to think of her as another granny.

Harri held up his gloved hand and clicked his tongue. Tân glided over to him and buried his head in the palm of the glove, looking for the worm he knew would be there. Tân tossed his head back, swallowed the worm whole, and flicked his tongue around his lips in appreciation.

'He might be a handful,' Harri smiled, tickling Tân under the chin, 'but I wouldn't be without him.'

'Mr Davies will be here with his tribe of Ancient Britons soon,' Imelda said. 'You'd better get yourselves ready.'

The two boys were dressed up as Ancient Britons, ready to play their part in the town's May Day Parade.

'Are you sure you know what to do with Tân?' Imelda asked.

'I'm sure.' Harri nodded.

'We don't want anyone to know he's a real dragon.' The old lady furrowed her eyebrows. 'They'll want to put him in a zoo or do experiments on him.'

'I'll help Harri,' Ryan said, earnestly.

Imelda didn't reply. She sucked her bottom lip and nodded slowly.

4

Chapter Two

Mr Davies

Mr Davies wore a huge smile as he strode up the street, leading his tribe of hairy Ancient Britons from their encampment in the park. They were going to head the May Day Parade.

Mr Davies had been elected Chief of the Wales and West Tribe of the Ancient Briton Re-enactment Society, who were better known as the Red Dragons. He was in charge at last.

Mr Davies loved history. At weekends, he and his wife and two little children would dress up as Ancient Britons and live in a leaking tent, eating cold porridge and turnips.

After dark, there's not a lot for Ancient Britons to do but drink lots of mead, which is a kind of ancient beer made with honey.

Then they get very merry and sing ancient songs

5

while Mrs Davies plays ancient tunes on her ancient harp.

Usually, at least one merry, hairy Red Dragon will trip over in the dark and break an arm or a leg. The hospital is quite used to bearded, hairy Ancient Britons with burns, broken bones or bleeding bits, arriving by ambulance on Saturday nights!

Mr Davies was the only Red Dragon warrior without a beard. 'Ho-ha!' he ordered, waving his sword in the air. The tribe of bearded, hairy warriors came to a halt outside Merlin's Cave — the shop where Harri lived with his mum and Imelda.

The shop sold magic stuff — healing stones, tourist knick-knacks and bottles of water from St Gertrude's Well. Since Imelda had been living with them, they had been selling her homemade love potions, cures and magic spells too. Business had never been so good.

The little town of St Gertrude's, where they lived, was celebrating the 1400th anniversary of the day

that St Gertrude tripped and bashed her head against a rock. The rock had split in two. Crystal clear water had sprung from its heart and had flowed through the town ever since.

Mr Davies and the Red Dragons were leading the carnival procession through the town down to the well. The well's ancient church and buildings had become a tourist destination. People came from all over the world to see it.

Harri and Ryan walked over and joined the tribe.

'Hail, Harri and Ryan!' said Mr Davies.

'Hail, sir!' The boys chorused.

'Don't call me sir,' Mr Davies whispered. 'Call me Chief when we're in the Red Dragons.'

'Yes, sir — I mean Chief!' Harri stammered. As his form teacher at school, Harri had always called Mr Davies 'sir'. Calling him anything else didn't feel right, almost like breaking school rules!

Harri pressed the switch on a radio control unit. A red light flashed on. He looked at Mr Davies and raised his eyebrow as if to say, 'Now?'

Mr Davies nodded. His eyes were alight with excitement. Wait until the Red Dragons saw this!

Ryan carried a box with flames painted on it. As Ryan opened the lid, Harri pulled out a long, thin aerial and pointed it in Ryan's direction. The small, flame-patterned flag at the end of the aerial fluttered in the warm breeze.

'Up!' Harri ordered, pointing the aerial towards the sky.

8

Ryan's box shook and quivered. The tribe gasped as Tân rose gracefully into the sky.

'Oh!' Mr Davies frowned. 'It's bigger than I remember.' Did he know? Had he worked out that Tân had grown since he last saw him at the school competition?

Mr Davies shrugged his shoulders, and pointed down the street, calling, 'Forward the Red Dragons! On to St Gertrude's Well!'

A forest of flags and banners were hoist up above the mob of Ancient Britons. Each bore the emblem of a red dragon.

The Red Dragons held their hairy, bearded heads high and shook their flashing swords at the sky.

'Ho-ha!' They shouted in one voice. The Red Dragons had a flying red dragon leading them today. None of them suspected that is was real and not a radio-controlled toy!

Chapter Three

Ryan's Dad

Ryan's dad was bored. There was nothing to do. Ryan's mum was at an IT conference in Las Vegas and Ryan was out with Harri being an Ancient Briton. He'd made a great costume for Ryan, but as there wasn't a best costume prize he wasn't interested in going to the parade. History wasn't really his thing.

You'd never catch Ryan's dad sleeping in a leaky tent, eating porridge and turnips, drinking mead with hairy beardy types — not when he could lounge on the sofa, drinking coffee and eating chocolate digestives.

He'd finished Ryan's homework and cleaned the house, so there was nothing to do but watch TV until the grand prix started.

There was nothing worth watching. Flicking

through the channels just brought up endless cookery and antique shows.

'What the…!' He sat up straight and turned up the sound.

'…which happened fourteen hundred years ago this very day,' the cheerful programme presenter said. 'Ever since then, the healing waters have flowed from the Holy Well of St Gertrude's, so today the townspeople have come together to celebrate this historic occasion.'

The programme was coming live from the market cross in St Gertrude's. The townspeople were dressed up in all sorts of funny clothes. The TV reporter dived into the crowd, pointing the microphone at two grubby urchins.

'And tell me how you are celebrating today, boys?' she asked.

One urchin carried a flame-painted box, the other was pointing a remote control unit up to the sky. A flame-painted flag fluttered on the end of the aerial.

11

'We're flying our remote control dragon to lead the Ancient Britons on the May Day Parade,' one of the boys said, nervously.

'That's Harri!' Ryan's dad hissed. 'And that's Ryan next to him … on TV!'

Mr Davies pushed into the picture. 'It's a practice run, see?' he explained to the TV presenter. 'We're the Red Dragons and we'll be coming back in August to re-enact the Battle of St Gertrude's. That's when the Ancient Britons, under the flag of the red dragon, beat the Saxons back across the border into England.'

'Ha, ha!' the presenter laughed, ducking as Tân swooped down to attack the hairy microphone. 'Make sure you have that in your diary, folks. Sounds like it's going to be lots of fun!'

Ryan's dad flicked the TV off, put on his coat, put his keys in his pocket and marched off to town. Ryan had said he and Harri were going to dress up for the May Day parade, but he'd definitely not said anything about dragons!

Chapter Four

Once in a while, when Tân looked like he was getting a little bit too excited, Harri pointed the aerial at the box that Ryan was carrying and called, 'Down!'

Tân was well trained. He knew he'd get a nice, juicy worm once he was safely back in the box.

He'd explained to Mr Davies that he was changing batteries, but he was really calming Tân down and reminding him to fly just above the little army of Red Dragons and not do anything too fancy, that might draw attention and make people wonder how a radio-controlled model could look so real.

How had he ever let Mr Davies talk him into this? Someone was bound to realise that Tân was a real, live, fire-breathing dragon.

Fire-breathing? That got Harri thinking, *Oh no!*
Harri had awful visions of Tân setting fire to
people's hats and all the flags, that were strung
between the lamp posts in the street, bursting into
flame! 'Don't do the fire-breathing!' he whispered
into the box. 'Not here! We haven't got a licence!'

Chapter Five

'I'd like to see you after class, Harri,' Mr Davies had said one day. 'I need to talk to you about your dragon.'

Harri was convinced that Mr Davies had found out that Tân was a real dragon and not a radio-controlled model.

It had all started when Mr Davies had set the class a creative challenge. He'd offered a bag of Dragon Gold for anyone who could make a dragon fly for more than ten seconds.

Ryan always won the school competitions — or rather his dad did. Ryan's dad did everything for his son. This time he'd made a model of a Chinese J-20 Mighty Dragon Stealth Fighter Aircraft for Ryan to fly in the competition.

As Harri and Ryan both flew their dragons for

more than ten seconds, they were joint winners. Harri was thrilled. It was the first time he had won anything. Even coming equal first seemed amazing. And it didn't even matter that the bag of Dragon Gold was only chocolate money — he'd won!

But Harri *had* sort of cheated. Imelda had used magic to turn his dragon drawing into a real dragon … but making a model plane was kind of cheating too, wasn't it? It wasn't the kind of dragon Mr Davies had had in mind.

'You know I dress up as an Ancient Briton at the weekends, Harri?' he asked.

Harri rolled his eyes and tried not to laugh. 'Er, yes, sir.'

'We-e-ell,' he continued. 'My tribe of Ancient Britons are called the Red Dragons, see? I was telling everyone about your wonderful dragon the other day, and we wondered if you might fly it as our emblem at the May Day Parade?'

'Phee-e-e-w!' Harri breathed a sigh of relief. Was

that all? Then, moments later, fear clutched at him. Blood rushed to his head and the floor seemed to go a bit wobbly. He wouldn't be able to hide the fact that Tân was a real dragon, not if the whole town was watching.

'Er-er-er,' he stammered, desperately trying to think of an excuse. 'Er … it's broken, sir!' was all he could say.

'That's no problem.' Mr Davies smiled. 'There are lots of very clever people in the Red Dragons. We can help you to fix it. It would look wonderful to have our group of warriors being lead by a flying dragon!'

Mr Davies' eyes glazed over as he imagined himself, the new Chief, leading his little army with a red dragon flying above them.

'Er-er-er…' Harri's mind had gone into brain freeze mode. Why couldn't he think of a good reason to say no? 'Thank you, sir.' It was like someone else had said it.

17

Harri left the room with Mr Davies staring into the distance, imagining the glories that waited for him and the Red Dragons on May Day.

Harri could hardly sleep that night. If some great, hairy, bearded Ancient Briton came to try and fix Tân, he was going to find out that Tân was real and didn't need fixing at all.

Maybe he could train Tân well enough to behave himself at the parade?

The next day, bleary-eyed from lack of sleep, Harri told Mr Davies he'd mended his dragon and it was flying again.

'That's wonderful news!' Mr Davies cheered. 'The May Day Parade is going to be fantastic! Thank you, Harri.'

And Mr Davies had been right. The crowds cheered as they marched past, waving their swords and banners, singing Ancient British marching songs, led by their dragon emblem flying high and proud above them.

18

Chapter Six

Everyone pointed and marvelled at the dragon that swooped, soared and spiralled in the carnival atmosphere.

'It looks so real!' they shouted.

'It's amazingly lifelike!' called others.

'There's no way Harri could build that on his own,' muttered one person in the crowd.

Ryan's dad pushed and squeezed through the throng of people that lined St Gertrude's High Street. He narrowed his eyes, and watched the dragon, analysing every tiny movement that it made.

It was uncanny. Not only did the dragon look incredibly real but Harri was controlling it like a pro. It took real skill to fly a radio-controlled model like that.

Over the din of singing Britons and the brass

bands that following behind in the parade, Ryan's dad heard Harri shout an order.

'Down!' Harri pointed his aerial at the box that Ryan was carrying. The dragon descended elegantly and landed inside.

What followed next happened so quickly, you might not have noticed, but Ryan's dad did. Looking the other way, trying not to draw attention to

himself, Harri peeled open the top of his remote control unit, like it was a plastic sandwich box and took out a wriggly, stringy worm!

Something poked out of the flamed-painted box … a mouth?

The something took the worm between its teeth, tossed it into the air, caught it and snapped its teeth shut.

Ryan's dad stood frozen to the spot, his mouth hanging open, gawping like a fish.

'It's real!' he whispered to himself.

The light on Harri's radio-control box flickered and switched off. Harri hadn't noticed. He pointed the aerial towards the sky and called, 'Up!'

The dragon flapped its wings and rose into the air again. The crowd cheered and jostled, but Ryan's dad was lost, deep in thought, unaware of the noise around him.

'It's real!' he whispered again. 'It's blooming well real!'

'It certainly looks like it,' said the man next to him, who was carrying a small child on his shoulders.

Ryan's dad shook his head. The noise rushed in, filling his ears again as he came back to reality.

He noticed an old lady on the other side of the street. An old lady dressed up in a pointy hat and a green cloak. She was watching him.

Their eyes met and locked together.

22

Imelda Spelltravers

No one else noticed the old lady in the pointy hat and the green cloak. She had a way of making herself invisible. Not invisible so that you could see right through her, just invisible so that you didn't pay her any attention. It was even easier for her with everyone else being dressed up.

She was keeping an eye on Harri and Tân, making sure that Tân didn't give himself away.

She felt responsible for the pair of them. Sometimes, she wished she had never made Tân. She'd so needed someone to believe in her magic powers and Harri was so willing to help her. Tân was just a small present she'd given him on the spur of the moment. She hadn't really thought of the consequences of a young boy owning a dragon in the modern world.

But then her life had changed so much because of her gift. It was wonderful to have Harri and his mum in her life, to feel wanted and needed again.

23

Harri and Tân were inseparable. After Harri had caught dragon fever, a special bond had been created between the pair.

The crowd was caught up in the celebrations. No one was expecting a real dragon so nobody saw one, just a fabulous radio-controlled model. So she didn't need to worry too much.

'It's amazing what they can do with technology these days, isn't it?' The lady behind her said to her partner.

But then Imelda sensed that someone was watching Harri. A man that didn't fit in the crowd. He hadn't come for a fun day out.

She saw it all. She saw Harri slip a worm to Tân who snapped it up in that playful way of his.

Then she felt the man's eyes on her and she could see that he knew. She could tell that the knowledge would eat away at him, that he would have to find out more about Tân, that he wouldn't let go until he did. She knew that she would see him again … very soon.

It was time to disappear — to really disappear, the full invisibility kind of disappear. She pulled her cloak around her and … she just melted away. The crowd flowed in to take up the space where she'd been standing.

'What the…?' Ryan's dad shook his head and nearly swore.

The man next to him frowned.

Confused, perplexed, but excited that he knew something special that no one else knew, Ryan's dad pushed his way out of the crowd and walked home briskly, thinking, planning.

'That blooming dragon is real!' he told himself for the umpteenth time, as he put the key in the front door.

Chapter Seven

The parade wound its way down the hill to St Gertrude's Well. There were drum majorettes with a kazoo band, sounding like a hive of angry bees, a drumming group making an almighty din and dancing wildly, lots of people dressed up in colourful costumes, shaking tins and buckets at people, asking for charity donations.

All the different churches marched with their banners fluttering. An ambulance and a fire engine flashed their dazzling blue lights. A fire rescue control vehicle whooped its siren every now and then. A steel band swayed and jived on the back of the truck. It was followed by St Gertrude's Carnival Queen, who was dressed up as St Gertrude herself. She and her lovely attendants were joined by Mister St Gertrude's, the bodybuilding champion, who wore a very skimpy

knight-in-tiny-pieces-of-shining-armour outfit, that showed off his huge, rippling muscles.

When the parade reached St Gertrude's Well, a choir sang an anthem, as all the civic dignitaries lined up.

The mayor, in his golden chain, made a speech.

'What a wonderful day and wonderful celebration of our town's Patron Saint,' he began. 'Even more wonderful was to have our procession led by a dragon that looked so real we could almost be back in the fifteenth century!'

Harri froze. The mayor seemed to be looking directly at him. His shining cheeks glowed with enthusiasm. Harri didn't want anyone drawing attention to Tân. People would start asking questions!

So far, no one had said anything other than what an amazing model it was and how clever Harri was to have built it. Tân had done his job and Harri had made sure he was settled quietly in his box, feeding on the rest of the worms.

'As I revealed in my latest book,' the mayor continued, 'St Gertrude was also responsible for saving the town from the ravages of a marauding dragon. Legend tells that she tamed the dragon and had it live with her in Castle Gertrude, until the day she died. Copies of my book are on sale now in shops around the town.'

Phew! The mayor was just trying to sell his book. Harri had got away with it. No one suspected the truth. After all, if you saw a red dragon flying in the street, you'd think it was an advertising stunt or something, wouldn't you? At least you'd think there were strings holding it up or it had propellers attached.

As the clock struck midday, the crowd hushed and bowed their heads. The bishop, in all her fine robes, said prayers and flicked water from the Holy Well all over the crowd.

And then it was all over. People broke up into groups, chatting and laughing.

Harri and Ryan stood next to Mr Davies, patiently waiting for him to stop talking to the mayor. At last he noticed them.

'Oh! Are you off now, lads?' he asked.

'Yes, sir … I mean Chief,' Harri said.

'Well, thank you, Harri. That dragon of yours was the star of the show!'

'It was amazing!' the mayor agreed.

'It's just a model,' Harri said, nervously.

'I know!' Mr Davies laughed. 'But it looks so real and you fly it so well, I could almost believe it was alive!'

Harri didn't like the way the conversation was going. 'Thank you, sir, er, Chief!' he put his head down and made his escape. 'Come on, Ry!'

They had only gone a few paces when Mr Davies called out. 'Oh Harri?'

Harri froze. He could feel his heart thumping in his chest. This was it. Mr Davies had worked it out and knew the truth. Slowly he turned round and looked at Mr Davies.

'Sir?'

Mr Davies smiled and winked. 'See you in school on Monday, there'll be class credits for both of you!'

'Phew!' Harri breathed again. 'Come on, Ry. Let's go!'

Chapter Eight

'See ya tomorrow then, Ry?' The boys stood by the postbox on the corner of the street, by the library.

'I'll have to help in the shop this afternoon. It'll be busy today.'

'Yeah!' Ry laughed. 'See ya then. I'm going to change into some normal clothes.'

'You should wash your face too!' Harri giggled. 'It's covered in Ancient British dirt.'

'You can talk!' Ryan jeered, jogging backwards down the side road that led to his house.

The Red Dragons liked to look authentic, which meant that everyone had to rub their faces with a dirty brown, greasy cream to make it look as if they hadn't washed for months.

I wonder if they ever wash those great big hairy beards? Harri thought as he pushed open the old, heavy door of Merlin's Cave.

Merlin's Cave was busy. The town was full of tourists who all wanted souvenir bottles of water from St Gertude's Well. Imelda was helping out in the shop, answering questions about her magic potions and spells.

An American lady was studying a packet of herbs. 'And you say this helps you to concentrate in exams?' she asked in her twangy voice.

'Oh, definitely,' Imelda said. 'Brew it up and drink it like tea before an exam, and you'll remember everything you ever revised.'

'That's so quaint!' The lady laughed like a donkey. 'I'd get arrested if I told them that at customs at the airport back home!'

Imelda smiled patiently. Some people just didn't believe in magic. It was pointless trying to explain it to them.

She kept glancing nervously out of the window and down the street. Her mind was distracted. Where was Harri? He should be back by now. She wouldn't be happy until he and Tân were safely home again.

'There you are!' Imelda smiled and sighed with relief. 'Go and put Tân out in the back and clean yourself up. We don't want anyone asking questions about the dragon at the parade.'

'It's okay,' Harri said cheerfully. 'We were very careful. Everyone thinks Tân is a model.'

Imelda's face crinkled up. 'Let's hope so,' she said.

But deep down, in her heart, she knew there was going to be trouble ahead, and it was all her fault!

35

Chapter Nine

'Hi, Ry! Had a good morning?' Ryan's dad was busy laying the table for lunch.

'Yeah, great, thanks!' Ryan put his head under the kitchen tap and began scrubbing his face with washing-up liquid.

'You and Harri were on the TV.'

'Did you see us? Did you record it?' Ryan spluttered.

'No, but it'll be on the internet.'

Ryan patted his face with a towel and clambered upstairs to his room where he dumped his Ancient British costume and got back into sensible jeans and T-shirt.

As Ryan sat down at the kitchen table, his dad slid a plate in front of him with an exaggerated flourish. 'Compliments of the chef!' he announced.

'Yum!' Ryan's eyes lit up. 'Ikea meatballs and microwave chips! My favourite!'

Ryan's dad waited until his son had eaten a few mouthfuls then, all sweetness and innocence, just sort of making gentle conversation, he said, 'Harri's trained that dragon really well, hasn't he?'

'Mmmmm!' Ryan spluttered through a mouthful of chips. 'You should see it when Harri calls him and he flies right to Harri's glove and...'

The clock ticked in the silence as the penny dropped and Ryan realised that he'd been tricked.

'…er-er, I mean when Harri presses the home button on the remote control, then Tân comes straight…'

Oh no! He'd used Tân's name like he was real. There was no way he could talk himself out of this. His dad said nothing, but slowly popped a meatball into his mouth, letting Ryan tie himself up in knots of confusion and shame. Shame, because he had given away Harri's secret, probably the biggest secret he would ever be trusted with in his life.

Harri was his best friend. *When Harri finds out, he'll never talk to me again*, Ryan thought. Dad was never going to forget that Tân had blasted his model Chinese J-20 Mighty Dragon Stealth Fighter Aircraft out of the sky, or that he had been beaten by a mere boy.

Dad loved winning. But more than he loved winning, he hated losing. Luckily, because he was always careful to make sure he never started something he couldn't win, he rarely lost at anything.

But when he did lose, well… He never gave up until he had got his own back, until he got what he like to call, 'Justice!'

Ryan's dad waited until his son's shoulders slumped in defeat. There was no way out — no going back.

'So tell me,' Ryan's dad smiled in that thoughtful, *really wanting to know because he was really interested* way of his. 'Where did Harri get his dragon from? Tân, was it? Did you say his name was Tân? I mean, a dragon's not something you just go out and buy at a pet shop, is it?'

Ryan stared at his plate. Three meatballs remained. He'd lost his appetite. His mouthful of half-chewed chips tasted like dry cardboard. What could he do?

'I'd really like to know…' Ryan's dad let the silence do the work. The clock ticked on. The sound of racing cars drifted in from the grand prix on the living room TV. Birds sang, a lawn mower started

up in the distance, a bee buzzed lazily past the open window.

A thought drifted through Ryan's head. *This is what people mean when they say that silence is deafening.*

Ryan reached for his glass of water. He thought he would explode if he kept his silence a moment longer.

Chapter Ten

It was Monday morning and the playground was pandemonium as usual. Kids were running about, shouting, screaming, waving goodbye to their mums and dads.

Harri bounced up to Ryan and tapped him on the opposite shoulder.

Ryan fell for the simple trick and looked the wrong way.

'Hi, Ry. I thought you were coming round to the shop yesterday?' Harri chirped.

'Uh, yeah. I—I—I had to do something with my dad,' Ryan stammered.

'That's okay,' Harri laughed. 'The town was full of tourists and the shop was so busy. Mum had me helping out, packing bags. If I see another bottle of St Gertude's water...'

Mr Davies appeared in front of them. 'Hello, boys! That was great work you did on Saturday. People have been talking about your dragon all weekend, Harri!'

'See you in class,' Ryan mumbled, breaking up the trio and melting into the throng of children that were waiting for the bell that would let them into school for the day.

'Oh, yeah. Thank you, sir,' Harri said, distractedly. That was odd. Why hadn't Ryan stayed to talk with Mr Davies? He'd worked just as hard as Harri to fly Tân at the parade on Saturday. He deserved half the praise.

'It was amazing!' Mr Davies beamed. 'In fact,' he continued, 'we were wondering if your dragon could be our mascot at our big meeting in August, for the Battle of St Gertrude's. We're really going to whoop those Saxons and make them wish they'd never heard of the Red Dragons!'

August? That was years away! 'Oh, yes, sir,' Harri

said, hoping Mr Davies would have forgotten by then.

'Oh, magic!' Mr Davies grinned. 'There's the bell! See you in class, Harri!'

Magic? Did Mr Davies know? It was so hard keeping Tân a secret.

Chapter Eleven

 'I almost feel like shutting up the shop for the day,' Harri's mum sighed, as she threaded a new roll of till receipt paper into the cash register. 'That was such a busy weekend.'

'I can look after the shop for you.' Imelda smiled. 'You deserve a day off.'

'Really?' Harri's mum thought of all the things she could be doing other than restocking the shelves and waiting for customers. There never were that many customers on a Monday.

She could be having a day out in the sunshine shopping! Ever since they had been selling Imelda's magical potions, the shop had been making real money. Maybe she could treat herself to some new shoes? Maybe she could get a present for Imelda to say thank you?

Imelda almost pushed her out of the door. 'Off you go!' she insisted. 'You spend far too long cooped up in this shop. Go and have a few hours to yourself.'

Harri's mum felt she was being really naughty, like she was sneaking off school, but it was wonderful to be out in the sunshine, free, with nothing to do but go and look around the shops. She could call it research! See if she could pick up any new ideas from other shops — why, that was almost like work! That made her feel much better.

Imelda closed the door and pottered around the shop, tidying and filling up the empty shelves. It was wonderful to be useful and wanted.

* * *

 In the library across the road, Ryan's dad chose a computer magazine. He got himself a cup of coffee and sat down in the window seat.

He hadn't been to the library for a long time. He read everything on his Kindle these days and if he needed to know anything, well, you just look it up on the internet, don't you?

They'd smartened up the library, though. And you didn't used to be able to get coffee. He might come again. They had a good collection of magazines and they were lending ebooks now. He'd have to ask and see how to do that.

But what was more important was the view outside the window. Across the street was the dry cleaners, next to that was the charity shop, and next to that was Merlin's Cave.

The row of shops was over a hundred years old and the red brickwork was a bit crumbly in places. Merlin's Cave had once been a chemist's shop. The large windows were decorated with a border of smaller panes of coloured glass.

It was very old fashioned, but somehow it seemed suitable for a shop selling magic. He was beginning

to believe in magic. How could he not? He had the evidence of his own eyes. That dragon was real!

Harri's mum was just coming out of the shop as he sat down. She wore a big smile as she turned her face up to the sun. She slipped up a side alley and soon reappeared, driving her car.

Good! Ryan's dad smirked. He watched her pull out and drive off towards the big shops on the edge of town. *She'll be on her own now!*

He finished his coffee and put the magazine back in the rack.

As he left the library, he picked up a leaflet in the foyer.

'Download library books to your Kindle or tablet,' it read.

He folded it carefully and slipped it into his back pocket as he crossed the road to Merlin's Cave.

Chapter Twelve

 Harri unpeeled his banana and took a bite. Ryan had joined in the football kick-about at the other end of the playground. Ryan was avoiding him. He kept looking the other way in class and not answering Harri's questions.

Megan and Lexi mooched over to him.

'Alright, Harri?' Megan asked.

'Mmmf!' Harri said, through a mouthful of banana.

'Saw you in the parade on Saturday. Your dragon was amazing — did you really make it all by yourself?'

Quick! Change the subject! 'You were with the Carnival Queen, weren't you, Lexi?'

Lexi laughed. 'Yeah! We were soaked when that bishop lady flicked water all over us!'

'I didn't recognise Mr Davies, at first,' said Megan. 'He looked so weird all dressed up as that Ancient Briton thing he does.'

Ryan had just scored a goal and was running round the playground, his shirt tail hanging out, punching the air as if he had just won the World Cup.

'Not playing football with Ryan, then?' Megan asked.

The bell rang for the end of break. 'No,' Harri said quietly. He lined up at the front of his class's row. Ryan, red-faced and out of breath lined up at the back.

Chapter Thirteen

 The doorbell tinkled in a friendly fashion. It was easily a hundred years old. It suited the shop. It was part of its history. How many generations of customers had come tinkling through those doors over the years?

Before Harri's mum had opened Merlin's Cave, as well as being a chemist, the shop had been a cobbler's, a printer's and a video rental shop.

'Come in,' Imelda said quietly. 'I've been expecting you.'

The man closed the door gently and looked around. He'd not really noticed Merlin's Cave before. It wasn't the sort of shop he'd ever needed to visit. What did people buy in shops like this?

Imelda watched as the man picked things up, studied them and put them back down again.

Not many men came into the shop on their own, they were usually with their wives or girlfriends. They often looked out of place and a little uncomfortable being there.

There are two kinds of magic. The type you see on the TV — all show business and fluttering white doves, done by men in top hats and twirly moustaches — and then there is the other kind of magic — quiet magic, Earth magic, that is mostly women's work.

'You're Ryan's dad, aren't you?' Imelda asked.

'And you must be Mrs Spelltravers,' said Ryan's dad. 'Ryan's told me all about you.'

Imelda held out her hand. 'Call me Imelda.'

Ryan's dad ignored the gesture and folded his arms. 'I've come about a dragon.' It was almost a whisper.

Imelda nodded. 'I thought as much.' Behind the heavy green velvet curtains that separated the shop from the storeroom and the rest of the house, something rustled.

'I want one!' Ryan's dad growled. 'I want a dragon.'

Imelda pointed to a couple of shelves where models of dragons were displayed. This was Wales, home of the dragon, and tourists loved buying dragons as souvenirs. Some of them had *A Gift from St Gertrude's* printed on them.

Since the mayor had written his local history book, and had uncovered the legend of St Gertrude taming a dragon, a little model of a dragon encircling a beautiful woman had become their bestseller.

The model was meant to come as part of a set with St George on a white horse, but as he didn't fit in the story, the manufacturers were happy to sell them on their own and change the words on the side from *St George* to *St Gertrude and the Dragon*. Tourists loved them.

Ryan's dad looked at the shelves, tutted and shook his head. 'I mean … I want a *real* dragon.'

52

The heavy green velvet curtain twitched.

They held each other's gaze for a long time, assessing each other's mental strength, both surprised at how good their opponent was at this game.

The curtains shook and quivered. A low growl filled the silence of the shop. Imelda and Ryan's dad ignored it, still staring each other out.

Imelda was the first to look away. Something moved in the edge of her vision, attracting her attention. Something red and shiny.

It leaped into the air and hovered above the herbal remedies. Its leathery wings, cracking and flapping, whipped the air into a chilly draught. A tiny wisp of smoke trailed behind it.

The creature pulled back its head and opened its mouth wide. Its eyeballs slid back into their sockets, protecting them from the yellow, fiery jet of flame that roared from of its nostrils like a flame-thrower.

Ryan's dad fell to the floor, covering his head with his arms.

53

Imelda ordered, 'Tân! NO!'

Tân dropped onto the cash register, standing guard over the unwelcome visitor. A final wisp of smoke trailed into the air as he extinguished the fires in his belly.

'Tân!' Imelda spoke in a quiet, measured tone. 'Leave us. Go back to your box right now. I can handle this.'

The little dragon hopped to the floor and shuffled backwards towards the storeroom. He never took his eye off the man until Imelda drew the curtains closed behind him.

'I want a dragon!' Ryan's dad growled, heaving himself up off the floor. 'I could have been scarred for life just now! I could have been killed by that — that — that — Tân! I want a dragon or else I'm going straight to the police, and you know what they'll do, don't you?'

Ryan's dad bared his teeth in a smile. 'Harri's precious dragon will be put in a zoo, kept behind

55

bars to keep the public safe. We can't have dragons roaming around setting fire to everything, can we?'

Imelda was between a rock and a hard place. Harri would be heartbroken if Tân was taken away. It was all her fault. She should never have created Tân in the first place. Dragons were always trouble, one way or another.

Her eyes dropped to the floor. Imelda had just run out of choices.

'I need a drawing of a dragon,' she whispered. 'Draw it yourself — it must be your dragon. Don't come back here. I'll come to you tomorrow at midday. Now go!'

The bell tinkled, its once friendly sound seeming hollow and shrill.

Ask not for whom the bell tolls, Imelda remembered the words of a poem. *It tolls for thee.*

56

Chapter Fourteen

Mum was so happy and busy showing Imelda her new shoes, she hadn't noticed the slight sadness in Harri's eyes. But when Harri had come in at the back door after school and found them both in the kitchen, Imelda had seen it. There were so few customers they'd shut the door and closed the shop for the day.

Imelda put her nose into the giant bouquet of flowers that Mum had bought for her, and took a deep breath. 'They are beautiful!' she said for the sixth time. 'Thank you so much. I really should put them in some water.'

'And look what I got for you,' Mum giggled. She handed Harri a stripy paper bag. 'Well, it's not for you, it's for Tân really.'

Harri put his hand into the bag and pulled out a

shiny, golden dog collar. It was studded with imitation plastic rubies.

'It's got a name tag and all!' Mum said. 'I'm afraid the machine couldn't engrave the accent over the letter "a", though!'

Harri turned the golden disk over. Sure enough, the letters 'T-a-n' had been engraved into the metal.

'It's great, Mum! Thanks.'

'Well, come on! Let's see if it fits. I think its really meant to be for a poodle or a Yorkshire terrier.'

Harri sat down in the armchair by the cooking range. Tân, pleased to see him back from school, jumped onto his lap to see if Harri had any special treats for him.

'Hold your head up,' Harri told him. 'And… Oh yeah! That is soooo cool! Tân, you look amazing. Thanks, Mum! Say thanks, Tân.'

Tân made a little bow and snuffed — a word that Harri had made up to describe the sound Tân made

when he was excited — sort of half sneeze and half puff.

Mum's good mood was infectious. Soon they were all cheerfully helping to make tea. Harri peeled potatoes and Imelda, with tears streaming down her plump cheeks, chopped onions, while Mum cooked and told them about all the amazing things she'd seen and all the ideas she'd had for the shop.

'The lights!' Mum said. 'They do amazing things with lights in those big stores. I'm sure we can do something here, make the place look just a little bit more magical. Lighting helps to set the mood. And smells too, here, what do you think of this?'

She rummaged in her shopping bags and pulled out a can. She sprayed a fine mist into the air. 'Fruits of the forest, it's called. What do you think of that?' she demanded.

'All I can smell is onions!' Imelda sniffed.

Chapter Fifteen

'Night, Ry. Sleep tight.' Ryan's dad turned out the light in his son's bedroom.

'Dad?' Ryan called from in darkness.

'Yeah?'

'Oh, never mind. Night night.' Ryan closed his eyes and thought about Harri and Tân. He knew that he'd destroyed their friendship. Harri was his only real friend too. He'd never get to play with Tân again. Not now.

Ryan's dad settled himself down at the kitchen table. He'd found an old pad of drawing paper and a battered set of coloured pencils in the cupboard under the stairs.

On the way home, he'd popped into the library

again and renewed his membership. He'd found two excellent books about dragons. They now lay open in front of him. Fantastic illustrations showed fearsome teeth and claws. One of the illustrations was so real, it could have been a photograph.

Ryan's dad drew the image he wanted again and again, tracing, copying, refining his drawing until at last, just after eleven, he was finally happy with his work.

He held the drawing up and smiled.

'Let's see what you think of that, Imelda Spelltravers!' he jeered.

Chapter Sixteen

 The next day at school, nothing had changed. Ryan was either avoiding Harri or ignoring him. What had Harri done? Why was Ryan behaving like that?

Harri spent most of breaktime talking to Jack and Ben, which was okay, but Jack *did* go on and on about all the horror films that he'd watched. Some of the descriptions made Harri feel quite creepy.

The day dragged on like any other day, except that Ryan didn't want to be part of it.

That night, Imelda poked her head round Harri's bedroom door. 'Night night, Harri,' she whispered.

Harri's *Star Wars* bedside light cast a gentle pattern of stars across the ceiling. Tân shuffled about at the bottom of the bed, trying to get comfortable. Dylan, Harri's cat, had got the best position.

'Night, Imelda,' Harri smiled, sleepily.

'Everything okay at school today?' the old lady asked.

'Mmm,' Harri nodded. 'Well, no, actually, Ryan's acting weird. He's stopped talking to me. It's like he's avoiding me. I don't know what I've done wrong.' Tears welled up in his eyes.

Imelda sat down on the edge of Harri's bed and took his hand. 'It's all my fault.' She sighed. 'I should never have got you involved with dragons, but then … maybe it was meant to be.'

'What do you mean?' Harri's face crumpled into a confused frown.

Imelda shrugged. 'Dragons can have a powerful effect on some people, and the effect they have depends on the nature of the person. You're a lovely boy, Harri, and Tân is a lovely dragon. He's sweet-natured and funny, like you, but he's also fiercely loyal … like you.'

Tân rolled over and flopped his head on the covers. Dylan lazily opened one eye and humpfed.

Harri laughed and tickled Tân under the chin. 'He knows we're talking about him.'

Tân blinked and snuffed, as only he could.

'Do you think Mr Davies has been affected?' Harri asked. 'I'm worried he knows the truth about Tân.'

'Oh yes, he's been affected alright!' Imelda chuckled. 'He's besotted with the whole idea of dragons, especially red ones. But he's so besotted with the idea, he can't actually see the real one that's right in front of his face!'

Should she tell him? Honesty *is* the best policy — little white lies always end up in a tangle of big, fat lies and mistrust.

'It's not Mr Davies I'm worried about,' she began. 'It's … it's Ryan's dad.'

'Ryan's dad?' Harri looked confused.

'He knows about Tân.' There, she'd said it now.

Harri's jaw dropped, his mouth hung open and hot patches of red glowed on his cheeks as the implications sunk in.

'Has Ryan told him?' Harri hissed through gritted teeth. 'He swore he would never tell anyone.'

'You mustn't blame Ryan,' Imelda said, gently. 'His dad is a very clever man. He knows how to persuade people to do and say things. I'm sure he can get Ryan to do anything he likes.'

Harri punched his fist into the duvet. Tân and Dylan leaped off the bed and hid inside the wardrobe.

'I'm never going to speak to him again!' Harri said.

'Never say never,' Imelda soothed. 'Ryan is probably feeling pretty sick with himself. I'm sure he didn't mean to tell about Tân. His dad would have made him talk somehow. I saw his dad at the parade on Saturday. He saw you feeding worms to Tân.'

Worms? Tân decided it was safe to come out of the wardrobe and jump back onto the bed. If someone was talking about worms, he wanted to be where the action was.

There were no worms, but the spot where Dylan had been sleeping was free. Tân sunk into the dip in the duvet that still held Dylan's warmth. He shrugged his wings and settled down to sleep.

'I think Ryan probably needs your friendship now more than ever,' Imelda went on. 'And I have a feeling you are going to need his friendship too. Very much.'

Harri didn't like the idea of losing Ryan as a friend but…

He closed his eyes and buried his head in the pillows. Harri was a forgiving boy, not one to bear grudges. Imelda was right. Ryan wouldn't have told his dad unless he really had to.

Harri sighed deeply. 'Night, Imelda. Thanks for telling me. At least I know I haven't done anything wrong.'

Imelda brushed a golden curl away from Harri's eyes. 'Of course you haven't.'

She stayed with him for a while as his breathing

became more shallow. The frown on his face faded into a peaceful, gentle smile.

Dylan jumped silently onto the bed and curled up next to Tân.

'Night, night, Harri. Sleep tight.' Imelda gently closed the door behind her as she crept out onto the landing. 'Night, Tân. Night, Dyl.'

Chapter Seventeen

 The clock in the hall chimed twelve times for midday. A moment later, almost as if it were a thirteenth chime, the doorbell rang.

'She's punctual!' Ryan's dad muttered to himself, shuffling across the hallway in his slippers and unlocking the heavy front door.

Imelda stood on the doorstep in her pointy hat and long green cloak. She carried a basket covered with a red checked tea towel.

Ryan's dad nearly laughed. She looked like something out of a fairy tale. In fact, she looked like that character in the kid's books Ryan had won in school last year. He'd sold them on ebay. What were they called? *The Happy Witch*?

Imelda didn't wait to be invited in. She stepped into the hallway and took command of the situation.

'Let's get on with it, then,' she said briskly. 'Let's have the drawing. You did do a drawing, like I said?'

'Err, yeah!' Ryan's dad was surprised. It was his house, but she was in charge. He led the way into the big kitchen and pulled the drawing pad out of a drawer. The drawer closed itself with a quiet, expensive, satisfying bump.

'Come on, show me!' Imelda clicked her fingers impatiently. She wanted this over and done with as quickly as possible. She was buying time now so she could work out what to do later.

The only colour on the drawing was the blue crayon in the sky behind the creature. 'It's a white dragon you're wanting, is it?'

Ryan's dad nodded.

'Are you absolutely sure you want to go through with this? Dragons are tricky creatures.' Imelda fixed him with her pale blue eyes. 'Whatever happens, it will be entirely your responsibility.'

This was a business transaction, he didn't want to get involved in chit-chat.

'I'm sure,' he said gruffly.

Imelda uncovered her basket, revealing an egg and a bottle of brown, gloopy liquid lying on a bed of straw. She removed the egg and unscrewed it.

Ryan's dad was amazed. His face looked much the same as Harri's did the day Imelda first came to the shop and began this whole dragon business with a magic egg just like this one.

She took the drawing and scrunched it up into a ball and, just as she had done with Harri's drawing, she placed it gently inside the bottom half of the egg.

Ryan's dad watched, open-mouthed, as Imelda placed the two halves of the egg together. The egg twisted, screwing itself back together, slowly turning round and round. The egg glowed for a moment, wobbled slightly, then came to rest on the kitchen table.

It was a perfect egg. Its surface was smooth and

there was no sign of a join or that it had ever been in two halves.

'How did you do that?' he gasped.

She shook her head and looked at him as if he were a simple, ignorant child.

'It's magic!' she snorted.

Ryan's dad felt small and stupid. He picked up the egg. It was warm and heavy. Moments ago, it had been a hollow shell with a piece of paper inside.

'You will need to keep it warm for about a week to ten days,' Imelda instructed in her brisk, efficient tone. She handed him the bottle. 'And you'll need to take a tablespoon of this everyday. Now, if that's all, I must be going. I'll see myself out.'

It took a few minutes to realise what had just happened. If that was magic, there hadn't been any spells or incantations nor any smoke or flashing lights. She was either winding him up or … she really was a witch and he was a holding a real, live dragon's egg in his hand!

71

It had all happened so quickly. Had she really screwed the egg together?

He made a nest with kitchen towel in an old ice cream tub and placed it on the sunny windowsill to keep warm. Then he searched online for those things they use for hatching chicken's eggs. His fingers flew across the keyboard until he found what he was looking for — they were called incubators.

An advert came up for a chain of country stores. There was one on the edge of town. He'd driven past

it a hundred times but, not being a farmer, he'd never gone inside. He phoned the store to see if they had any incubators in stock.

'Yes, sir,' the bored-sounding girl had told him. 'We've got all the different sizes in at the moment.'

It hadn't taken long to drive there and get one, and it hadn't taken long to set it up in a locked cupboard in a secret corner of the garage.

He opened the bottle of brown liquid that Imelda had given him and sniffed it.

'Pfwaah!' It was revolting! What on earth was in it? Was she trying to poison him? Was that her game?

He hid the bottle behind the incubator and locked the cupboard door. Evidence! If anything went wrong, he could use the witch's poison as evidence against her!

Chapter Eighteen

Harri wrote on a piece of paper, then he folded it over three or four times, so no one would open and read it, then he wrote Ryan's name on it.

When Mr Davies turned to the whiteboard and started pointing out how the semicolons were being used in a poem, Harri nudged Megan and gave her the message.

The message slowly worked its way across the classroom. From Megan to Lexi to Ben to Rhys and finally to Ryan.

Ryan looked round and frowned. He unfolded it and read the message under his desk. His head jerked round. His and Harri's eyes met. Ryan looked … scared? Guilty?

'Would you like to share that with the class?' said

Mr Davies, who had quietly sneaked up on Ryan and whisked the message from his hand.

'Let's see, what does it say?' Mr Davies read the message, then he repeated it out loud to the class. 'I — know — your — dad — knows... Hmmm. That's very interesting, Ryan. What *exactly* does your dad know?'

The rest of the class giggled. Ryan turned bright red. In his confusion he couldn't think what to say.

'Ryan's dad knows everything!' Ben said, cheekily.

The class erupted in laughter. Ryan was almost in tears.

Mr Davies looked uncomfortable. He hadn't meant to humiliate Ryan.

'Now now!' he called the class to order and handed the message back. 'Put it away now, Ryan. What have I said about passing messages in class?'

'No passing messages in class, sir,' the children chorused.

'Exactly!' Mr Davies turned back to the

whiteboard to take the focus off Ryan. 'Now who can tell me why the poet uses a semicolon in the third line down?'

After school, Harri waited for Ryan at the gate. The boys ambled down the street, side by side, until the pack of mums and dads and children had dispersed and they were alone.

'I'm so sorry,' Ryan finally broke the silence. 'He tricked me, see? You don't know what my dad's like. He knew about Tân already — he'd seen you feeding him worms on Saturday and worked it out.'

Harri knew Ryan's dad too well. They had been battling each other for years, not one to one, but through Ryan. Through Ryan's homework, and projects and all the other things that Ryan's dad did to make sure Ryan came first or top of the class.

Ryan's dad had always been really nice and friendly, helpful even. But then, he'd never lost before.

'Dad's gone a bit weird,' Ryan said. 'He spends all

his time locked up in the garage. I don't know what he's doing in there. I wish Mam would get back from America. It feels like she's been away for ever. She'd sort him out.'

Ryan stopped and stared at the ground. 'I don't think he's going to be happy until he's paid you back for shooting down his plane.'

Harri felt his stomach lurch. That wasn't fair! He was just a boy. How could he defend himself against a grown man?

'I hope we can still be friends?' Harri said quietly.

Ryan looked up. A tiny smile of hope spread across his face.

Neither of them had to say a word. Neither of them knew what to say anyway. But something unspoken had created a new and stronger bond between them. Something deep and magical. Maybe it was something to do with being around dragons?

After all, Ryan had spent quite a lot of time with Tân. He must have been affected by dragons too.

Chapter Nineteen

'What's the matter with him? Is he going to be okay?' Ryan fretted. He looked worried, his face was pale and drawn. 'Dad kept calling your name, telling me to go and fetch you.'

Ryan's dad tossed and turned in his bed. The bedclothes were soaked with sweat. Imelda felt his forehead. He was burning up. *Dragon Fever!* she thought.

'Where's your mam, Ryan?'

'China!' Ryan sighed. He could hardly remember when he'd last seen her, she was so busy running her IT business these days. The conference in Las Vegas had gone so well, she'd flown on to China to set up some new contracts.

'Should I get the doctor or an ambulance?' Ryan looked really worried.

'There's not much they can do.' Imelda smiled to reassure the boy. 'You were right to come and get me, Ryan. We'll get your dad well again in no time. Have you got some ice in the fridge? We need to cool him down.'

'The fridge has got an ice-maker in it,' said Ryan. 'I'll go and get some.'

* * *

Two days later, Ryan's dad opened his eyes. 'What the devil are you doing here?' he croaked.

Imelda held a glass of water to his lips.

'You didn't do as you were told,' Imelda said, gruffly. 'You didn't take the medicine I gave you. It would have protected you from dragon fever. Goodness knows what it's done to you.'

Ryan's dad's eyes widened, as he slowly remembered how he'd watched the egg hatch and how the tiny dragon had clung to his wrist, pricking

his skin with its tiny claws. 'Where is it? Is it okay?'

'I've been looking after it,' Imelda said. 'It's fine. It's waiting for its master to recover.'

'Ryan? What about Ryan?'

'He's at school. I've been staying in the spare bedroom and looking after him as well as you. He's been really worried.'

'Does he know?' Ryan's dad croaked.

Imelda shook her head. 'No, and I've not told anyone.'

Ryan's dad relaxed and fell back into the pillows.

'You'll be okay, now the fever has broken,' Imelda explained. 'I can leave you now. Keep taking this medicine.' She pointed at the bottle of brown gloop. 'And make sure you finish it all!'

Ryan's dad scowled at her from under his eyebrows and grunted. She knew it was all the thanks she would get.

Chapter Twenty

 It was a beautiful summer. It seemed that every day was filled with sunshine and bright blue skies.

Harri and Ryan spent the long, hot days wandering the hills above St Gertrude's. When the the coast was clear and there was no one about, Harri would open his backpack and let Tân out to fly along with them.

When Tân wasn't chasing rabbits, Harri was teaching him to follow commands and come back when he was called.

If they saw other walkers, Tân knew to drop down immediately, into the heather or a thick, prickly gorse bush, until they were out of sight.

'How's your dad?' Harri asked.

They were sitting on a rock, eating their crisps

and sandwiches. The town below them was like a toy model. It was market day and they could see people going about their business, bustling in the streets. In the distance, the sea sparkled and behind them, the mountains rose up to meet the scudding, pillowy clouds.

'He's okay,' Ryan nodded. 'But he's changed since his illness. He's quieter — he's gone moody. He's stopped doing stuff for me all the time, which is great. But sometimes, it's like he can't wait for me to come round to see you — like he wants to get me out of the house. Mam says he'll be back to his old self soon.'

Harri pulled a bit of ham from his sandwich and offered it to Tân. Tân stood on top of the rock, his head held high, his wings half open, standing proud like … well, yes … just like the red dragon on the flag of Wales!

Sometimes, Tân would stare towards the mountains, almost in a trance. Harri would follow

the little dragon's gaze and wonder what it was that drew its attention.

Dinas Emrys was in that direction, the place where the mythical dragons of the Mabinogion were buried deep underground.

Was that it? Was Dinas Emrys calling him? It was calling Harri. Every day, Harri thought about the trip he and Mum had taken there last autumn. He felt he belonged there. He didn't know how to put the feeling into words, so he kept quiet about it. But he knew it was important. Somehow his destiny was tied up with that place and the story of Merlin and the red and white dragons that were buried there.

There was only one dark cloud on the horizon: the Battle of St Gertrude's.

All summer long, Harri's promise to Mr Davies had weighed heavily upon him.

'He's going to notice that Tân has grown!' Harri said for the umpteenth time.

'We need to make a new box and we'll have to

make it look just like the old one,' said Ryan. 'Tân hardly fits in it anymore.'

'It's hard, keeping a dragon,' Harri sighed. 'Someone's going to find out about Tân one day, then I don't know what will happen.'

Ryan nodded, but he said nothing. His dad had found out. Why had he never mentioned it again? There must be a reason. He must be up to something!

Chapter Twenty-one

'We need to learn more about dragons,' Imelda told Harri one morning. 'Not just to help with looking after Tân. We need to know more about dragons. I don't know what is going on in Ryan's dad's mind.'

Harri and Imelda crossed the road to the library. He followed her up the stairs to the hushed sanctuary of the reference library. He'd never been up there before. Old books and boxes were piled on dark, carved wooden shelves. Large chests contained maps and documents. It smelled of old dust and wax polish.

The floor creaked loudly in the studious silence.

The mayor was sitting at a desk, surrounded by books and papers. He glanced up and smiled when he recognised Harri.

'Hello!' he whispered. 'You're the lad with the flying dragon, aren't you?'

Did he know? Did he suspect?

'Did you really make it all by yourself? You're very clever, you know?'

Harri smiled and said nothing, in case he said something he shouldn't.

'Come and look at this,' the mayor said, untying a green ribbon on some rolled-up parchment. 'It's very old. It's part of the town archives but it's written in a language I've never seen before.'

He spread out the document. 'Here — you'll like this little picture at the top.'

A boy and a woman stood in front of a castle holding hands. The woman held a jug from which water flowed into a stream. The boy's hair shone with real gold leaf. A red dragon, with flaming nostrils, stood on the walls of the castle tower. All around the picture, strange, curling words were written in fading ink.

Harri reached out. As his fingers lightly touched the document, a spark, like an electric charge, shot up his arm, making him jump.

'It's Emrys!' Harri whispered.

'Emrys?' the mayor sat up. 'You mean, Merlin? What makes you say that?'

The mayor looked at Imelda. Her lips were moving as her eyes scanned the words of the document.

'You can read it!' he whispered.

Imelda held the mayor's gaze a full ten seconds before she spoke. She decided she could trust him — they were going to need friends. The mayor was an honest historian, seeking truth in the past.

'It's written in the old language,' she explained. 'Harri's right. That's Emrys, or Merlin.' She pointed at the boy in the painting. 'And that is St Gertrude.'

'Merlin and St Gertrude knew each other!' The mayor gasped.

Harri could see it all in his head, like a movie playing before his eyes. He could feel the story reaching out across time, reaching out across hundreds of years … reaching out and claiming *him*!

'When the Red Dragon killed the White Dragon,' Harri began, 'no one could control it, not even Emrys, for he was still a boy. The dragon went on the rampage, destroying everything in its path. Now it was free, it wanted to remain free. Eventually, the

89

dragon came here, where St Gertrude met it and offered it a drink of water from her well. The mystical powers of the water tamed the dragon and Emrys gave it into her care.'

Imelda and the mayor listened to Harri, open-mouthed.

'That's exactly what's written in the document.' There was wonder in Imelda's voice. 'It also says that the king gave St Gertrude a special charter allowing her to keep a dragon in her tower.'

The mayor's eyes were wide with excitement. 'But that's incredible!' he gushed. 'There are piles of old documents in the archives, imagine if we could prove the story was true!' He winked at Harri. 'Your mother would be pleased. I'm sure it would bring more tourists to the town *and* to her shop.'

Imelda smiled and brushed a golden curl from Harri's eyes. *Emrys has returned*, she told herself for the second time.

Chapter Twenty-two

'Here comes the dragon, lads!' called Mr Davies. His hairy, bearded followers punched the air and cheered.

'Thanks for coming, boys,' Mr Davies smiled. 'You've no idea how much it means to us to have a dragon flying as our mascot. We're going to beat those Saxons good and proper!'

'Yo!' chorused the hairy, bearded warriors. 'Death to the Saxons!'

The Ancient British Re-enactment Society had set up camp at one end of the park, under the shadow of the ruins of Castle Gertrude. The Ancient Saxon Re-enactment Society had set up their camp down by the bowling green. The Ancient Saxons were just as hairy and bearded as the Ancient Britons.

According to the posters that decorated all the lamp posts for miles around, the battle was due to begin at 2.30pm.

By 2.25pm, a huge crowd had assembled to watch the show. Music trilled from a little funfair down by the pond while an announcer explained what was going to happen on the loudspeaker system.

'Welcome ladies and gentlemen, girls and boys. Welcome to the world of history, to a time when savage war was waged between the Ancient Britons and the bully-boy Saxons, invading from the East.'

The two armies lined up and raised their fists and shouted vile curses at each other. The crowd booed or cheered, depending on who they were supporting. The atmosphere was electric.

'Ready, boys?' Mr Davies puffed his chest out and pulled himself up to his full height.

Harri switched the light on his radio-controlled box and pointed it towards the new, much larger box. 'Dragon … up!' he ordered.

92

'It's bigger than I remember?' Mr Davies sounded surprised.

'I — I — err. I crashed the last one, Chief,' Harri explained. 'So I made a new one. A bigger one — a better one.'

'Fabulous!' Mr Davies grinned as Tân rose gracefully above them.

The hairy, bearded warriors cheered at the site of their emblem. 'Long live the Red Dragons!' they chanted.

The crowd cheered. They were really getting into the spirit of the occasion.

Then a murmur swept across the crowd. The murmur turned into an *Oooh!* and then an *Aahh!*

Harri couldn't believe his eyes. The Saxon army lay a hundred metres from them. Now above their heads another dragon flew! A white dragon! If anyone in the world knew about dragons, Harri did. This wasn't a radio-controlled model, this was a real dragon. *Where on earth had the Saxons got a real dragon from?*

93

The line of Saxons parted. A Saxon chief walked through the gap and stared directly at Harri! A sinister grin spread across his face.

'Ryan! It's your dad!' Harri gasped.

'What the…?!' Ryan was lost for words.

Ryan's dad held up a radio control unit. He too was pretending to be controlling a model dragon. 'Behold, Draca, the White Dragon of the Saxons!' he roared.

'It's 2.30!' The announcer could barely contain his excitement. 'Let battle commence!'

The two sides raised their swords and spears and shields and charged.

'Long live Draca! Long live the White Dragons!' yelled the Saxons, as they began their headlong stampede across the newly mown grass towards the Ancient Britons.

* * *

 Harri kept one eye on Tân and one on the white dragon, which was circling, gaining height above the marauding Saxons.

'Up, Tân!' Harri ordered. 'Get up high!'

It was too late. The white dragon tucked up its wings and fell from the sky like a rocket … like a rocket trailing smoke.

'Oh no!' Harri threw his fake control box on the ground. There was no point pretending anymore. He cupped his hands around his mouth. 'Tân! Watch out!'

It started as a trail of tiny, crackling sparks, then blazing, flaming jets of yellow fire shot out of Draca's nostrils. The crowd cheered. What a fantastic show! They hadn't expected dragons — they looked so real!

Tân flipped and rolled as he felt the flames scorch the scaly tip of his tail. Where had that dragon come from? He didn't look friendly, and he wasn't playing a game. This was a real fight!

The white dragon came at him again, flames blazing. This meant war! Tân closed his wings and dropped like a brick. He opened them at the last moment, swooping over the heads of the crowd.

96

'Oooooooh!'

The white dragon had anticipated Tân's move. It circled and came in for another attack.

'Aaaaaaah!' The crowd were loving it … until they realised the white dragon was heading straight for them with both nostrils blazing with heat and fury.

The roar of the flames could be heard above the spectator's screams as they ran in all directions.

'Stop it, Harri! Stop it now!' Mr Davies was shaking Harri's shoulders.

'I can't, sir — I mean Chief!' With all the tumult going on around him, Harri had remembered to call him Chief!

'Switch him off!' Mr Davies yelled.

'I can't!'

Mr Davis picked up the radio-control unit and flicked the switch on and off. As he did, the top came off the box and a pile of worms fell from inside it.

'What the … urrgh!' Mr Davies saw the fear on Harri's face.

97

'Oh my Lord!' he gasped. 'They're real! The dragons are real!'

Ryan's dad stood in the middle of it all, watching the mayhem, laughing like an evil genius from a bad cartoon movie.

Tân was not going to be beaten. Rage would not help him now, but anger would stoke the fires in his belly. He flew towards the sun, so the other dragon would be blinded if it tried to follow. He struggled to get higher … higher still, as the heat built inside him.

Feeling like his little heart was ready to burst, Tân turned and dived.

The white dragon was far below him. With the sun behind him, it couldn't see Tân coming.

The first the white dragon knew of the attack was the sound of Tân's fires igniting, the sputtering jets of flame building to full blast, then the pain as Tân burned a hole through the leathery fabric of its right wing.

The creature screamed. Unable to control its flight, the white dragon tumbled out of the sky, but

not before it lashed out, grabbing Tân by the tail, dragging him down, falling, falling through the air.

The canopy over a sweet stall broke their fall. They crashed onto the counter, snarling and growling, lashing their tails, slashing with their claws, scattering sweets in a cloud of gummy bears, flying saucers and smarties.

'Tân!' Harri ran towards them.

'Draca!' Ryan's dad was running as fast as he could too.

Police sirens pierced the frenzied row.

'Tân!' Harri ordered, 'Come here now!'

Tân held his head low, wings outstretched, ready to pounce in an instant. Waves rippled down his ribbed body as a low growl emanated from his belly.

'Tân! Now!' The rest of the world faded away. All Harri's concentration was focussed on Tân. Tân had to know that Harri was his master. 'I said now!' Harri hissed.

Tân dropped his wings a fraction, a sign to the

white dragon that this battle was over. But the war had only just begun!

Tân inched backwards carefully, warily, keeping his eyes firmly on the white dragon, in case it should still try and attack. When he was a safe distance away, he let Harri pick him up and hold him firmly in his arms.

Tân let out a sigh of relief. He flicked his tongue out and licked Harri's face.

'Well done!' Harri whispered.

Chapter Twenty-three

 'We'd like you to come along with us, young man,' said the police inspector.

Harri was surrounded.

The Police Dog Handling Unit had been giving a display in the park. A policeman wearing padded armour was approaching the white dragon warily. He carried a stick with a loop on the end. He placed it over Draca's head and pulled it tight. Then he led the struggling creature to his van where he manhandled it into a cage.

'Never had to deal with one of them before, sir!' the policemen told the inspector.

'That's my dragon!' Ryan's dad protested.

'Then we'd like you to join us at the police station too, if you don't mind, sir?' said the inspector, with a weak but professional smile. 'The general public

have been placed in grave danger today and they will want to know who is responsible.'

The dragon catcher was approaching Harri with his stick. Harri felt Tân's muscles tense, ready to protect himself.

'Quiet now, Tân,' Harri reassured his pet, clipping the lead to his collar. 'There's no need for that.' Harri nodded at the dragon catcher's stick. 'I'll put him in a cage, but don't put them in together — they'll fight.'

Warily, the policeman led Harri to another van. Harri placed Tân inside. He felt terrible as the policeman slammed the cage door shut. Tân looked confused. His big, brown eyes pleaded for an explanation as the policeman closed the back door, trapping Tân inside.

'Can I come with him?' Harri asked.

The inspector had never had to deal with dragons before and he hadn't had any training for situations quite like this. He nodded.

'I think you have a lot of explaining to do, young

man.' He turned to the other policemen. 'Get those … those things back to the station and keep them in cages while we work out what we are going to do with them,' he ordered.

'Go and tell my mum and Imelda what's happened,' Harri told Ryan, as he and Ryan's dad were put into the back of a police car. 'They'll know what to do.'

Almost invisible in the crowd, Imelda had seen the whole thing. All her worst fears had come to pass. What could she do? She was helpless. Everything was now in the hands of the law.

Chapter Twenty-four

'You are both being charged under the Dangerous Wild Animals Act of 1976. Do you understand?'

Harri and Ryan's dad stood in front of the sergeant's desk, heads bowed, as the station sergeant formally charged them both. 'Do you understand?'

It had all been explained to Harri. He'd been at the police station for hours. Because of his age, they'd had to wait for his mum to arrive with a solicitor. She and Imelda had sat in the interview room, while Harri explained everything to the inspector.

'Magic? You mean like witchcraft?' the Inspector asked Imelda, incredulously, when he'd heard the whole story.

'Not witchcraft. Not like you're thinking, all

Halloween and broomsticks,' Imelda said, shaking her head. 'It's Magic, see? The Old Magic — Earth Magic. Most people have forgotten all about it.'

The inspector didn't know what to do. He thought he'd witnessed everything possible during his career in the police, but this was something entirely new.

Harri was obviously a bright-eyed, honest boy, not the sort to get in trouble with the law. But people could have been hurt at the re-enactment battle and someone had to be held responsible. You can't let dragons breathe fire all over people! There are laws against that sort of thing!

'You will be arrested,' he explained. 'You will have to appear before the magistrates tomorrow morning. They can decide what happens next.'

'What about Tân?' Harri asked.

'That's up to the magistrates too,' said the inspector. 'Your dragon will have to stay here until then.'

'He gets very hungry,' Harri said. 'He likes worms best … and pepperoni pizza.'

'Don't worry.' The inspector smiled. 'We'll look after him.'

Chapter Twenty-five

 Mr MacDonald, their solicitor, blew his cheeks. 'Well, this is a strange case! I've not had to deal with anything like it before.' He'd come to the shop to escort them to the magistrate's court.

'The media and the TV are going to love this story,' he warned them, 'so be prepared for a bit of a scrum. Don't say a word. Don't answer any questions — not to anyone. We are going to have to play our cards very close to our chest.'

He was right. The re-enactment battle had been filmed by hundreds of people. Videos of people screaming and running away from the swooping dragons were online and had gone viral. Millions of people had watched them all around the world.

Satellite vans were parked on both sides of the

street. Reporters talked to their cameras in a host of different languages as Harri, his mum, Imelda and Mr MacDonald tried to squeeze through the doors of the magistrate's court.

'Harri! Tell us how you feel about having your dragon locked up?'

'Harri! Where did you get your dragon?'

'Harri! Did you mean to threaten the lives of so many people yesterday?'

'Harri! Have you got a girlfriend?'

The questions echoed all around him. Reporters thrust microphones at him, barging each other out of the way, all of them eager to get a snippet of news for this, their latest and greatest story.

'No comment!' Mr MacDonald kept shouting in a firm, authoritative voice, as he shielded Harri and guided him into the comparative peace of the magistrate's court.

His case was called quite quickly.

The room was lined in pale wood. Three

109

magistrates sat above them all. Mum and Imelda sat at the back, while reporters and onlookers strained to get a good look at the boy — *the boy with the dragon!*

The court clerk asked him to confirm his name and address.

'You are charged under the Dangerous Wild Animals Act 1976,' the clerk announced. 'In that you did recklessly allow a wild animal, namely a dragon…' A murmur went round the court. It was true!

The clerk coughed loudly and continued, '…namely a dragon — to roam free and unleashed and that you did put people's lives in danger. How do you plead?'

Harri wished the floor would open up and swallow him. He never meant to hurt anyone, neither had Tân. It was all Ryan's dad's fault!

He heard a voice making a speech. It was his voice! He'd spoken before he knew what he was going to say.

'Dragons have a right to live at St Gertrude's Tower. There's a royal charter that says so!'

Harri felt his cheeks burning red with embarrassment and defiance. A gasp spread around the courtroom.

Mr MacDonald stood up and coughed loudly. 'Err-hum! I beg the court to excuse my client. This is a very stressful occasion for him. He does not wish to plead at this moment.'

The magistrates discussed the case with the crown solicitor, whose job it was to persuade them to find Tân and Harri guilty.

I haven't done anything wrong! Harri thought. He was close to tears. This was all some terrible mistake. Maybe he would wake up soon and it would all turn out to be a bad dream?

'This case will resume in two weeks time,' the chief magistrate announced. He looked over the top of his glasses and studied Harri. 'We feel it is unlikely that you will go on the run, young man, so you are free to go home on bail. In the meantime, for the protection of the public, the dragons, Tân and Draca, must be kept under lock and key at the police dog pound, while their fate is decided.'

* * *

Home was like a prison. The reporters hovered outside the shop, interviewing anyone who went

112

in. The shop had never had so many customers before! Most of them were just being nosey, asking questions and buying souvenirs.

Harri was all over the internet and the TV and the newspapers. Groups of giggling girls came in the shop asking for his autograph!

Once a day, Harri was allowed to visit Tân and take him treats. But each time he went to the police station, it meant facing the cameras and more questions.

When Tân saw him, he would run up and down his cage, snuffing and snorting with pleasure to see his master again. But he would slump to the floor and plead with his big, sad eyes when it was time for Harri to go.

Draca paced restlessly in a cage across the pound, snarling at Harri as he was escorted back out to the street and the waiting reporters.

Harri couldn't bear to watch the news. Some angry people said terrible things about Tân and Draca.

They wanted them destroyed immediately — they said dragons were unnatural. Some people suspected that the dragons had escaped from a laboratory where they had been created by mad scientists!

After a few days, things quietened down a bit. Then the red ribbons began appearing on the lamp posts, followed by the stickers and the posters:

Free St Gertrude's Dragons!

The mayor was on their side, leading his own campaign. This story was good for business and the tourist trade in St Gertrude's.

Chapter Twenty-six

'And so, the Crown recommends that, after proper scientific investigations, the beasts be destroyed immediately.' The crown prosecutor was putting her case to the magistrates.

Members of the public had been queuing all night to watch from the public gallery. They wore 'free the dragons' T-shirts and badges. They shuffled their feet and murmured their disapproval. What horrible experiments would *proper scientific investigations* involve?

'We don't know how large these creatures will grow, nor do we know how dangerous they will become. They *cannot* be allowed to go free,' the prosecutor concluded.

There was a disturbance at the back of the room. The mayor was having a loudly whispered

conversation with one of the court officials. He was pointing at Harri.

Everybody followed the mayor's gaze and stared at Harri as the official came towards him and held out some rolled up documents.

'The mayor says you might need these,' the official explained.

As Harri touched them, the same charge of electricity shot up his arm. He knew this was the document about Emrys and St Gertude. There was another document with it. The court held its breath. In the silence, the ancient parchment creaked and crackled as Harri carefully unrolled it.

Harri wasn't sure but he thought it was written in Latin.

At the bottom of the parchment, a huge red wax seal hung from a ribbon. The image of a king on a throne was pressed into the sealing wax. He saw the word 'Rex' — probably the only word of Latin that Harri knew. *Rex means King!*

Harri couldn't speak Latin, but he instinctively knew what this document was. He stood up and held it above his head. He took a deep breath and spoke slowly and clearly.

'This is the royal charter allowing dragons to live at St Gertrude's Tower!'

The courtroom erupted in a confusion of loud and excited conversations.

The chief magistrate banged his gavel on the table and called all the officials to the bench for a discussion. The crown solicitor frowned as she read the document once, twice and then a third time before nodding her head and going back to her seat.

You could hear a pin drop as the magistrates whispered together, deciding what to do. They called the mayor. The mayor smiled and nodded enthusiastically as they asked him questions. Finally, the chief magistrate made some notes on a pad and faced the court.

'This is an unusual case,' he began. 'Without doubt, the royal charter is authentic and it means that the dragons had every right to be at the re-enactment of the battle of St Gertrude's. The park was originally part of St Gertrude's Tower. We have no choice but to release the dragons from police custody.'

Cheers erupted from the gallery.

Harri couldn't cheer yet. Mr MacDonald put a reassuring hand on his shoulder.

119

The Magistrate continued with his verdict, 'However, the dragons represent a clear danger to the public. They will be placed in the charge of the town council and must be kept in St Gertrude's Tower at all times. If they are ever found outside the town walls, they will be destroyed immediately.'

He turned to Harri. 'As for you, young man, we feel that you are not responsible for the mayhem caused at the re-enactment of the battle of St Gertrude's. That blame lies elsewhere and will be dealt with later. Obviously you can't keep your dragon as a pet anymore, so you will have to surrender ownership of your dragon to the town council. You are free to go.'

Cameras and microphones were thrust into his face. The questions came fast and furious as they left the court.

'What's it like to lose your pet, Harri?'

'Where exactly did you get your dragon from, Harri?'

'How did you know about the royal charter?'

'How do you feel, Harri?'

Harri didn't know how he felt. He'd seen Ryan in the courthouse, waiting for his dad to go in and hear the verdict in his case. Would they let him off so easily?

Would he ever see Tân again? What would he do without him? These questions rang loud in Harri's head. *Was life even worth living without Tân?* He and Tân had grown close over the short time they had been together. No one would ever truly understand … there is a special, magical, secret bond between a dragon and its master.

Chapter Twenty-seven

 The TV satellite vans were out in force again, the day the new St Gertrude's Tower Dragon Experience opened.

Ryan's dad slumped on the sofa and watched the whole thing on the TV.

'Why don't you go into town and join in?' his wife suggested. She was worried about him. He'd not been the same since she'd got back from China — he was so moody and grumpy. He spent all his time watching TV. 'It looks like everyone's having a brilliant time up there?' She smiled, hopefully.

Her husband curled his lip and grunted quietly. The court had made him pay a huge fine for causing all the trouble at the battle of St Gertrude's. He didn't mind that — they could afford it. But he couldn't get over the fact that Harri had beaten him again,

and he'd had his dragon taken away. The law may have spoken, but he wanted justice!

No one would ever truly understand how he felt … there is a special, magical, secret bond between a dragon and its master.

'Look!' Ryan's mum pointed at the screen. 'There's Ryan and Harri and Mr Davies, their teacher!'

Mr Davies and the Red Dragons were marching along with their hairy, bearded pals, the White Dragon Saxons. The Carnival Queen and her attendants were dressed up again as St Gertrude and her merry friends, and Harri was going to be guest of honour, cutting the ribbon to officially open the new Dragon Experience.

There were dragons everywhere — on T-shirts, on tea towels, mugs, caps, flags and posters. You could buy dragon cakes, dragon pasties and dragon pizzas, and a special dragon ale was on sale in all the pubs. Dragon pennants zig-zagged across the street.

The mayor made a speech and told everyone about his new *History of Dragons* book. Signed copies were selling like hot cakes in Merlin's Lair.

The band played and finally, the TV cameras got to see the dragons.

Harri spent the day showing Tân off to one camera crew after another, answering the same questions over and over. 'But tell us, Harri,' they kept asking, 'where did you *really* find him? You don't expect us to believe that magic egg story, do you?'

He told them the truth, again and again, but no one believed him.

 When it was all over and everyone had got their stories and told their tales, Harri snuggled down in the straw with Tân. He was exhausted. He could feel Tân's heart pounding against his soft, scaly skin. Harri talked gentle words of encouragement to Tân and Tân talked

back in his strange language of snuffs and squeaks and rumbles.

The dragons were on separate floors in Castle Gertrude to '*double the experience!*' Tân was kept in a dungeon kind of dragon's lair with old-fashioned prison bars caging him in. This was going to be his life from now on — gawped at by strangers six days a week, with Mondays off.

Harri was allowed to see Tân for half an hour every day at closing time, to feed him and keep him clean — no one else wanted to go into a dragon's lair and do the job alone.

It was better than nothing. It was better than losing Tân forever or having him put down, but they were never going to wander free again — running across the hills above the town, chasing rabbits, looking for worms and learning new tricks. Would Tân ever be allowed to fly again?

Suddenly, Tân sat up straight and stared intently through the narrow slit window of his dungeon. His wings quivered and a long, low growl rippled through his body.

'What is it, Tân?' Harri followed the dragon's gaze. Someone was darting about, down by the entrance gates to the castle — someone who was trying not to be recognised by the security cameras,

someone with a hood up and a scarf covering half their face.

It wasn't much of a disguise — Harri recognised Ryan's dad instantly by his jacket and the way he moved.

Ryan's dad was stapling a poster to the entrance sign. The poster was mostly black decorated with a white dragon and white lettering that said:

Free the Dragon.

Ryan's dad stood defiantly before the tower. Harri wasn't sure if he could see them through the tiny window, but he felt the anger and frustration coming at him like a laser beam.

Harri had never wanted Ryan's dad as an enemy. They shared something that no one else could ever understand, the secret bond between a dragon and its master. Harri knew that Ryan's dad would never give up until his dragon was free.

The words of the poster went round and round inside his head, stirring him up like a virus.

Free the Dragon.

Free Tân!

'I'll never give up,' Harri whispered in Tân's ear. Tân tilted his head. His huge yellow eyes fixed him with a look of purpose and hope. 'I'll never give up until we are free!'

Can Harri save Tân?

Find out soon in their next adventure,

Dragon Red, by Shoo Rayner